Time for Sleep

Written by:
Alyssa Wilburn

Illustrated by:
Tabitha Hamm

To order additional copies of this book, contact:
Xlibris
844-714-8691
www.Xlibris.com
Orders@Xlibris.com

ISBN: Softcover   978-1-6641-6020-0
         EBook   978-1-6641-6019-4

Print information available on the last page

Rev. date: 02/23/2021

Time for Sleep

My little baby, go to sleep

It's time to rest so please don't weep.

While you rest have sweet dreams of

Floating clouds and gentle streams

And if those streams move too fast,

Mama's going to take you to the past.

And if the past becomes too dicey,

Mama's going to take you to a place that's spicy.

And if that spicy place is too small

Mama's going to take you where the trees grow tall.

And if the trees refuse to grow,

Mama's going to take you to a Broadway show.

And if that Broadway show can't amaze,

Mama's going to take you to a galaxy far away.

And if that galaxy doesn't have enough space,

Mama's going to put you in her happy place.